NEW TO WORLD

SERIES 1

MEHARAZ.H

To all children who have felt different. To the person who has struggled a lot to achieve their dreams

Contents

Foreword

- **Hello**! My name is Meharaz. h *so I'm just a little girl with big dreams my dream is to publish my book. Never thought that my dream will come true just because of nationpress.com. I'm really thankful for this website. HOPE you will like my story................. .....MEHAR*

Preface

Most of the struggles that occurred in this book are experiences of my own. I just want to enjoy this world with my pains but life is so unpredictable and always gave me so many struggles to go through. But I'm a fighter I will fight till my last breath...............

Acknowledgements

When I will *try to tell the story of Zoya's life I will completely cry out. It's very emotional to tell about her she is just new to the world with lots of hope in her eyes to enjoy her life.....................*

Prologue

- **IT is a story of a girl named Zoya.** This story tells the complete history of her life .... When Zoya turned 16 her family forced her to get married to the guy who was her uncle...

CHAPTER ONE

Zoya's Birth

*In the year 2004*August 25, it was the middle of the night a pregnant lady was admitted to TAMIL NADU's government hospital for her first delivery her parents were standing outside of the room praying for her normal delivery. On *August 26* early morning it was time for sunrise when the sun was just above to raise there was a crying sound in the hospital it was a sound of a newborn girl baby. The nurse informed to lady's parents that their daughter gave birth to a GIRL child. After listening to nurse lady's father was disappointed because he was expecting that his daughter will give birth to a boy but unfortunately it was a GIRL CHILD. He gave money to his wife and told you and your daughter to come in auto he left the hospital out of anger. So sad of the girl baby she was just new to world no one welcomed her or no one was happy what was her mistake? HER mistake was she was born in the wrong world in a wrong society where people use to like BOY CHILD, not GIRL children. Well, when the lady's mother entered the room she informed her that she gave birth to a girl child the lady was happy to know that she gave birth to a girl child she told to nurse to show her the baby. The nurse gave the child to her she kissed the child on the forehead and said

to the baby 'THANK YOU FOR COMING IN MY LIFE".

CHAPTER TWO

First meet with dad

28TH August The lady and her child were discharged from the hospital they came back home but there was no one to welcome them inside the house because the lady's dad was upset he went and sat in his sister's house. The lady's mother went inside the house and welcomed them. TRING TRING the phone call rings A man picked up the phone call and said 'Hello' on the other side the lady speaks 'Hello Ji I and our child is safe we are in my mother's house you come soon here' the man was happy and with excitement, he asks his wife ' Tell me girl or boy ' his wife tell's ' Its surprise come soon to know ' and the call ends. 30 minutes later KNOCK KNOCK someone was knocking the door the lady's mother opens the door the man enters the hall and ask with his mother-in-law ' Kaha hai wo log ' she reply's ' Andhar room mai hai ' the man run inside the room and hugs his wife and take the baby in his hand his wife tells ' Beti hai ' the mans eye started to fill with tears of happiness he tells his wife ' Thank you for this little princess ' it was a different feeling for both of them to see their first child and now they has big responsibilities of their daughter . The man was telling to the baby ' I wish I will be able to fulfill your dreams in future you dont worry dad and mom will be

there always with you to support and protect you I just wish you grow up soon and call me papa'

CHAPTER THREE

Naming ceremony

29th August The whole family was gathered and the relatives were coming to see the newborn child and to give her a beautiful name everyone was busy in chit-chatting and seeing the baby girl. But someone's eyes were looking out of the door like they were waiting for someone to come to the party the lady keep a hand on the shoulder of the man he turns back she asks him ‘ Kiska wait for kar rahe ho ’ he tells her ‘ I'm waiting for mom to come actually she is not happy that its girl child she is angry she told me that she won't come for the ceremony but I told she has to come for my sake ‘ the lady's tells ’ Don't worry she will definitely come because loves you so be relaxed come and suggest some name for our baby‘. The people started suggesting so many names that time lady's father tells that ’ My mother's name was Zoyain so I would like to name my granddaughter Zoya ' everyone agreed with his words the man slowly whispers in the baby's ears three times Zoya, Zoya, Zoya the baby smiled. Suddenly the sound comes near the door am I late for the ceremony it was the sound of a man's mother she walk inside the hall and come near to the baby. She accepted the child just because she saw happiness on her son's face.

CHAPTER FOUR

1st year birthday of Zoya

The year 2005 August 26th, it's been one year today and it was Zoya's 1st-year birthday everyone was busy decorating the house Zoya's father was so much happy he just wanted to do everything perfectly and he informs his wife that ' After the cake cutting we should leave to the Chennai today because my owner is calling me telling that tomorrow I should be in work ' wife agrees with him. It's the afternoon the cake has been delivered. Zoya was ready for the cake cutting she was looking so pretty in the pink gown just like a princess. Cake cutting was done Zoya's father said to his mother that he and his family has to leave today for Chennai but his mother didn't agree with his words she said ' Today is Zoya's birthday and we didn't celebrate properly but your telling you want to go ' he said that it's urgent he can't stay. But everyone was disappointed about what to do Zoya's father was helpless. The argument continued till evening at last everyone agreed with Zoya's father the packing was done they left home and reached the railway station. The train reached platform number 5. It was the first journey of a Zoya. Night 11oclock they reached Chennai

they came home and slept out of tierdness.

CHAPTER FIVE

Zoya's first day of school

The year 2006 is early morning Zoya's mother was waking her up for her first day of school. Zoya's mom was so much nervous because it was her daughter's first day in school she wanted everything to be done perfectly she ironed her uniforms and polished her daughter's new shoes made her daughter a bath and feed her breakfast she packed Zoya's favourite biscuit in her lunch box. She gave a lunch box to her husband and said ' You drop Zoya in the school" her husband said 'I won't drop her because I can't see my daughter crying' he said that and went to his work. Zoya's mother made her daughter ready and took her school bag and started teaching her how to talk with teachers they went to school by walk. They reached the school the teacher came near the gate to pick Zoya up for her class when she carried her up Zoya started crying when her mother saw that she is crying she was not able to control her tears she sat near the gate road. She knew her daughter will be back to her in a few hours but she was a mother and only mothers will understand her feelings. Zoya was not able to understand where she has come she was around many children who were crying to meet their parents Zoya just wanted to know which place will she be able to go back to her family. Zoya's mother didn't go back home she was near the gate only waiting for her daughter. The time passed the school bell rang every kid was coming out of the school finally Zoya came out she ran and hugged her mother.

CHAPTER SIX

Zoya's sister birth

In the year 2007 December 31st was the day there was a new member came into Zoyas's life, her mother was admitted to the hospital for her second delivery but Zoya didn't know about it she thought her mother is going to die she was crying very badly her father next to her and said nothing to be worried your mother is fine she is just going to give a birt the other baby he asked whether you need a girl or a boy she said I don't know I want my mom to be safe. It was afternoon the crying sound came from the hospital room the nurse came out of the room with a girl child she gave the child to Zoya's father he showed that baby to Zoya she was so much happy she wanted to carry the baby but her father didn't allow her because she was only 5 years old. Her sister was been named Naziya she was born so much beautiful that she looked like Monalisa. Now Zoya has a girl sister now Zoya was the elder daughter of their family. Well, next what happened Zoya will tell us.

CHAPTER SEVEN

Shifting to Banglore

In the year 2010 **HELLO! I'm Zoya today we need to shift our things to BANGLORE from CHENNAI we are shifting just because of some issues. I don't belong to a rich family IM from a middle-class family my dad is a plumber, electrician, and carpenter and he knows to put puncher to... So now we don't have enough money to rent a house in a Banglore city so my dad knows one of a rich man in a Banglore he said him about our problem's he offered my dad a Watchman work he gave us a small room in that building the room was so much small only 2 peoples would be able to live there but we didn't have any other option then adjusting in that small room. We are 4 members and my mom is pregnant too we were in a difficult situation. I have never seen so high buildings in my life and I didn't even understand the language of Kannada I just thought only 3 languages exist in the world [Urdu, Tamil, English] but I was wrong there are so many languages which I didn't know. We struggled a lot with some days we didn't even use to get proper food 3 times a day. My sister Naziya was only 3 years old she use to feel hungry she use to cry for the food but we were helpless there were a people very HI-FI the kids of their will play in the road I and my sister** use to see them playing but they didn't join us they use to see us like a dog they use to feel that if we touch them they will become dirty they use to run far from us just like we were monsters. I just hated this city I thought good people won't exist in this city but I was wrong there was a building opposite our house there use to live one family even they were watchmen to they had 2 daughters similar to our age elder sister name was Kanchana and younger sister name was Guna we became a good friend later my sister got one more friend named Asha. After a few months, we got admission to the same school in Kanchana and Gunas. That day was my first day of school I was nervous but I was happy because I and Kanchana were in the same class I thought she will be with me but I was wrong her attitude changed in school she was feeling ashamed of me she use to talk about me with other girls in Kannada and laugh I was heartbroken I stopped talking with her even near the house. A few days passed like this then I got two good friends Gayathri and Vaishnavi they both were very good they always supported me Gayathri had an elder sister in the same school she was 7th standard she use to like me she thought me how to speak Kannada after some days Khanchana felt bad about her behaviour she apologized with me I forgive her and we all became good friends. A few months passed in the year 2011 August 17 my mom gave birth to a boy child a new member came into our life his name was Mohammed Abbas the family was completed now. After some years Khanchana and her family wanted to shift to their village they went again I was all alone. My dad opened a puncher shop he called his brother to stay with us his brother know to put puncher his dad opened a tea shop next to that shop and he called his Father-in-law to take care of that shop. I have changed my school my life was going on the happiest track my father's brother name was Saruvath Ali I use to call him chicha.

CHAPTER EIGHT

Death of chicha

In the year 2014, **We all has come to ANDRA PRADESH to attend the marriage of our relatives we all cousins are enjoying a lot we were having so much fun I just love my native place everything was normal and superb. It is a morning today was NIKKAH I woke up and came out of the house there was a crying sound from all I thought they were crying just because their daughter will go far from them after the marriage but the matter was different my cousin brother [Nafees] came to me and said that chicha met with an accident I thought he was trying to prank me I said by laughing stop your joke it's not funny. But I saw tears in his eyes I got to know he was not lying my heart was not ready to accept the truth I said to him please tell me that I'm dreaming or tell me that you're pranking me but he was quiet I just felt like time has been struck my chicha has 2 small children 1st daughter can't walk and 2nd was a boy he was just 1 year old and his wife was pregnant too. We all went to TAMIL NADU to my grandma's house my chicha was admitted to [GH hospital] in CHENNAI. It has been 6 days but he was not able to fight against death he use to cry when he see my dad. He wanted to say something to my dad but till the end, he didn't say and he was no more. I can't even** explain how much I liked him I never thought I would lose him so soon. But I should accept the truth and move on after his death we came into a bad situation. When we came back the owner told us to leave the house in 2 days we didn't even have money because every money was spent on chicha's operation but the owner didn't understand our situation we shifted our house to another building that house was big one room hall kitchen and attached bathroom was there this house we got from the help of my mother's friend even I have changed my school but I was not able to forget my chicha I got so many new friends [Chaitra, Kalaivani, Ishika, Shifa, Veda Valli, Malar] life was going in a normal way.

CHAPTER NINE

Twist in Zoya's life

In the year 2020, I'm 16 years old I was proud of my parents because my cousin and sisters got married in small age but my parents supported me in studying I was glad. I'm 10th standard now I'm really in fear because this time I will be having board exams and I have not understood any of lessons the because online classes are going on Coronavirus is there but I have lots of hope with Coronavirus HAHAHA! but I should study I know I shouldn't be careless. My whole life I struggled a lot but I hope this year will be the best. But life never let me be happy I didn't expect this from my parents my parents are forcing me to get married to a guy who is 13 years bigger than me and in my lifetime I had called him uncle. He doesn't have hairs on his head I don't like that guy.....

TO BE CONTINUED....................

Zoya Will Marry Him?

- *Zoya will continue her study or she will marry that person.*
- *Or someone will help her?*
- *Why she doesn't like him does she love another boy?*
- *Will she be able to achieve her dreams?*
- Support me to succeed in this book I will write another book about Zoya's marriage or About her decision.
- The story is based on true life........
- To be continued the story in the NEW TO WORLD series 2

9 798887 838779

Printed by Libri Plureos GmbH in Hamburg, Germany